# Magic Ballerina™

## Jade and the Enchanted Wood

# Darcey Bussell

HarperCollins *Children's Books*

*To Phoebe and Zoe, as they are the inspiration*
*behind Magic Ballerina.*

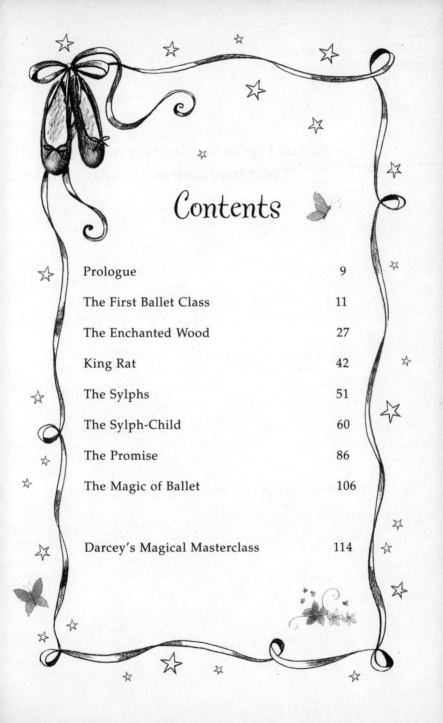

# Contents

# Prologue

In the soft, pale light, the girl stood
with her head bent and her hands
held lightly in front of her.
There was a moment's silence and then
the first notes of the music began.
For as long as the girl could remember
music had seemed to tell her of
another world – a magical, exciting
world – that lay far, far away.
She always felt if she could just
close her eyes and lose herself,
then she would get there.
Maybe this time. As the music
swirled inside her, she swept
her arms above her head, rose on to
her toes and began to dance...

# The First Ballet Class

Jade was half skipping, half jogging down the road, clicking her fingers and flicking her wrists. She hardly ever just walked normally these days. That would be too boring.

It was a beautiful Saturday morning,

sunny and bright. Inside her head music was pulsing, and the strong beat filled every part of her body. It felt great. But then she realised she was getting very near that house with the brass plate on the door: *MADAME ZA-ZA'S SCHOOL OF BALLET* and her feet began to slow. Why ever had she thought to come here? It just wasn't her. She tried to imagine herself in the ballet class, wearing a leotard and tights, her hair scraped back in a bun, the red shoes on her feet...

The red shoes! A little surge of

excitement whizzed through Jade's body. It was the shoes that had set her off on this whole ballet thing. Someone had left them in a parcel on Jade's doorstep with a note attached. Jade could remember the words exactly, she'd read them so often.

*Dear Jade,*

*These shoes are for you. I know you love dancing and I really hope you find out how special they are. Madame Za-Za's ballet school is just down the road and she is a brilliant teacher. Go and see her – and take the shoes. You won't regret it. I promise.*

And ever since the afternoon when she'd received the shoes, she'd turned over and over in her mind what had happened earlier that day.

She had been in her front garden, showing her two little sisters some street dance moves, when suddenly she'd realised that a girl was watching her. The girl had told Jade that she was a brilliant dancer, and asked if she did ballet. Thinking about that now made Jade feel embarrassed. She'd replied very rudely – saying that everyone who did ballet wore silly little tutus.

14

Jade knew she shouldn't have said
that, but she'd felt annoyed at the
time. Why would she like ballet just
because she loved street dancing?
Ballet looked so stiff and awkward.

You couldn't just let the music carry you along.

That's why it had been such a surprise to find the shoes. If they were so special why would someone give them to her when she didn't even like ballet?

Anyway, there wasn't time to think about that now. She'd decided to give it a chance and her mother had phoned ahead and booked her into a trial lesson. As she stood at the bottom of the steps that led up to the big front door, she breathed in deeply.

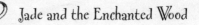

Just after ten o'clock. She was a little
bit late. Still, she patted her bag with
the red shoes in it and told herself for
the hundredth time that she was only
staying for one lesson to see what was

so special about it. Then she leaped up the steps, two at a time, and peered in through the big front window.

The class had already begun. Fourteen girls, wearing identical leotards, stood holding a wooden rail that ran around the walls of the room.

All of them were making exactly the same slow careful movements. Jade rolled her eyes as she came away from the window and pushed open the heavy front door.

Once inside, she caught sight of the changing rooms immediately. The door was ajar. She changed into her red shoes and pulled her hair into a bun. She already had her leotard on under her clothes so at least she wouldn't make herself even later by getting changed. Then, whispering under her breath, "Right, let's get it over with,"

she made her way to the ballet studio
and pushed open the door.

Madame Za-Za broke off her
counting when Jade walked in, but
the girls kept on doing their exercises
in time to the music. They seemed to
be pointing their feet to the front,
then the side, to the back, then the
side again. A puzzled look passed
over the teacher's face, but then, as
her eyes flickered down to Jade's
ballet shoes, she broke into a smile of
recognition.

"You must be Jade! Welcome. I was

expecting you. We've
already started, but
come on in."

"Sorry I'm late,"
Jade muttered
under her breath as
she quickly took her
place at a space on the
wooden rail.

"Place your hand lightly on the
*barre* – so."

Jade did as she was told, feeling the
darting glances from all over the class.
"Follow Chloe…"

"Er… I've never actually done ballet before, Madame…"

"Not to worry," Madame Za-Za spoke quickly. "I have a feeling you'll soon pick it up. Straighten the legs. Heels together—" Madame Za-Za was correcting Jade as she spoke, lifting her arm, lowering her shoulder and tilting her chin up. "And soften the wrist… Yes, that's it…"

*This feels ridiculous*, Jade thought. But the music was playing and everyone had started the exercise, so she followed as best she could, feeling

herself growing more and more tense
as Madame Za-Za kept correcting her.
"Relax the arms, Jade!"

How could she relax her arms when every other part of her body was tense? She looked across at the other girls to see if they had noticed, but luckily they were too busy concentrating on their own positions. And they were all so good at it. *Much better than me*, thought Jade. Then it crossed her mind that if they tried street dancing for the first time like she was trying ballet, they might not find it so easy.

"Eyes to the front, Jade, and turn out the supporting foot!"

Feeling frustration flood through her, Jade suddenly snapped. "Why do you have to follow all these rules? That's not dancing! Look! *This* is dancing…"

And she did a moon walk, followed by a leap in the air, then some quick footwork she'd only learned that week, her wrists flicking in front of her

as her body rocked from side to side.
She could hear gasps coming from all
around. Everyone looked across to
Madame Za-Za to see what she'd say…

# The Enchanted Wood

There was a silence for at least ten seconds, then Madame Za-Za nodded slowly, a thoughtful look in her eyes. "You have dance in your soul, Jade," she said quietly. "And somewhere in that soul of yours there is a place for

27

ballet too. We just have to find it."

Phew, at least she hadn't been told off, but it didn't help her to enjoy the rest of the class any better. It was "point this, straighten that". In fact her whole body was itching to forget ballet with all its rules, and just dance freely. How much longer was this lesson going to go on for?

Jade glanced at the clock. Ten twenty-eight. Over half an hour left. If only she could have a break. Just for a few minutes to shake all the tension out of her body. Well, perhaps she *could*…

Jade and the Enchanted Wood

"May I go to the loo?" she asked
politely.

Madame Za-Za nodded and Jade
hurried into the corridor. Stretching
her arms up, she flopped them over,
laughing quietly to herself. But her
amusement stopped
abruptly. Something
strange seemed to
be happening to
her feet. Was it her
imagination or were
her little red shoes
glowing? No, it definitely

wasn't her imagination. Now they were sending a tingle through her whole body too.

Suddenly, she was surrounded by swirling, whirling colours. Could this be what the note had meant when it said the shoes were special? Jade felt her heart race with excitement as she rose up off the floor, spinning and whirling in a blur of rainbow colours…

Suddenly everything stopped swirling and Jade found herself in the middle of

a quaint-looking village square.

She looked around her. "Where am
I?" she whispered. Her immediate
thought was that it all felt like a dream,
so she pinched herself. No, it was
definitely real.

"Hello! Hello!"

Jade looked round and saw a white cat, in a golden waistcoat and a top hat, leaping up to her. Stranger and stranger!

"Welcome to Enchantia!" the cat said. His kindly eyes twinkled as he looked at Jade's shoes, then at her face. "You're the new owner of the magic shoes!"

*Enchantia? Magic shoes?* Jade looked down at her feet. What was he talking about? But before she had a chance to ask any questions, the white cat had jumped high into the air and criss-crossed his feet at the ankles a few times before landing lightly and holding out a soft white paw to shake hands. "I am the White Cat, at your service."

"I... I'm Jade."

"Pleased to meet you, Jade. I guess you know why you're here in Enchantia."

*Enchantia?* There was that funny word again. Jade's eyes widened. "Well, not really…" she said.

"Aha!" The White Cat reached for his tail and whirled it round, which made Jade giggle in spite of herself.

"Well, whoever owns

the magic shoes in the real world is brought to the land of Enchantia when we need help," he explained. "It's where all the characters from the ballets live."

"Ballets? But I don't know anything about ballets!" Jade said.

The White Cat grinned. "I don't believe that for a moment," he said. "Come on, let's walk and talk."

"OK..." Jade said hesitantly, still unsure of what exactly was going on, but excited all the same. "So, where are we walking to?" she asked.

"The Enchanted Wood," said the
White Cat.

Jade liked the sound of that.

"Enchantia is a wonderful place to
live," the White Cat said. "We all love to
dance, well, with the exception of King
Rat." The cat pursed his lips disapprovingly
and continued in an anxious tone,
"Actually, it's because of King Rat that
you're here. He wants to build a funfair
in the Enchanted Wood, you see!"

"A funfair!" Jade
grinned at the White
Cat. "Sounds great!"

"Well no, it's not so great, I'm afraid." The cat was looking very serious now. "The Enchanted Wood is a place for everyone at the moment, a peaceful place we can all go to dance. King Rat's funfair would be just for him, so where would we all go? And it's not only that – a group of sylphs live in the wood. They would have to find themselves another home too."

Jade didn't know what the White Cat was talking about. "Er… what exactly *are* sylphs?" she asked politely.

"You don't know?" A distant look

came into the White Cat's eyes.

"Sylphs are the most beautiful ballet dancers ever," he replied. "Shy creatures who keep themselves to themselves." He turned to Jade. "When they dance, they light up the whole place with their magical white light which is what makes the Enchanted Wood so special for the rest of us."

Jade actually thought the bright
lights of the funfair sounded a lot more
exciting than some kind of light from
a group of dancers, but she didn't
suppose that was quite the thing to say
to the White Cat. She clearly wasn't the
right person to be the owner of these
magic shoes. But now the White Cat
was looking at her again.

"Can you help us?" he asked.

Jade gulped. She had no idea what
on earth she could do, but the poor
White Cat looked so forlorn, she
nodded. "Maybe I can talk to King

Rat?" she suggested hesitantly.

But again she must have said the
wrong thing, because the White Cat
shook his head violently. "Oh, my
 shimmering
whiskers and
glittering tail!" he
exclaimed. "Jade, you
must understand, King Rat is really
dangerous!"

Jade's eyes flew open. Why did the
White Cat sound so panicky?

"Shall we carry on walking to the
Enchanted Wood then?" she suggested

tentatively, trying to change the subject.

The White Cat tipped his head to one side. "Or better still, let's get there super fast!"

And with that, he drew a circle with his tail on the road and told Jade to step inside the magic ring.

A moment later, they were surrounded by spinning silver sparkles that lifted them high up in the air…

# King Rat

"That was so cool!" gasped Jade as her feet touched the ground. Then she looked up at the mass of tall dark trees that stretched as far as she could see. "So this is the Enchanted Wood!" she breathed.

The palest creamy light seemed to be drawing her into the wood and she hurried forwards, then stopped. "Oh!"

A large sign had been suspended from one of the trees:

PRIVATE PROPERTY. KEEP OUT! TRESPASSERS WILL BE IMPRISONED!

Jade shivered. Surely signs like this usually said *trespassers will be prosecuted*. And that just meant paying a fine, didn't it?

"There! You see what I mean!" said the White Cat. "King Rat is a nasty piece of work!"

"He certainly sounds it, but—" Jade
broke off as the most horrible rat she
had ever seen suddenly came stalking
out from the wood. He was wearing a
purple cloak and
golden crown
and had
black greasy
fur. Seeing
them, he
pulled out
his sword. It
had to be King
Rat!

"Are you blind?" King Rat snarled, two beady eyes staring out at them. His breath stank and Jade took a step back. "Or is it just that you are so stupid you can't read?" he went on. A long hooked claw on the end of a thin paw was stabbing the air in the direction of the sign. "*Keep out!* it says."

"I was only looking!" Jade replied, sounding braver than she felt.

The White Cat bowed, his eyes on the ground. "I'm so sorry, Your Majesty. This is my young friend's first visit to the Wood and she… er… didn't notice the sign."

Jade watched King Rat, sneering down his snout at poor White Cat, and felt cross. This might be a king standing before them. But only a *Rat* King, and a very rude one at that!

A second later, his beady eyes were back on her again. "You look like one of those wretched sylphs!" he said accusingly. "If I ever catch any of them, I'll have them locked up in my dungeons. I'm not having a band of silly creatures getting in the way of my

funfair!" He was spitting a bit so Jade
edged gingerly to one side.

"Time for us to go now, Jade," the
White Cat said, tugging on her hand
with his silky paw.

But King Rat clearly had other ideas.
He looked suspiciously at Jade, his neck

jutting out, his red eyes in slits.
"Perhaps you *are* a sylph yourself! I've
never seen you around. You're
obviously in disguise, but that tied up
hair and your silly way of standing
like a ballet dancer are a bit of a give
away!" The snarl turned to a screech.
"Guards! Capture them!"

"Get down Jade! It's a lasso!" yelled
the White Cat.

A loop of rope was flying through
the air, fast approaching. Jade dropped
to the ground just in time.

"Watch out!" she yelled. But it was

too late. The White Cat was caught in
the tightening rope.

"Run before he gets you, too!" he
shouted fearfully. "Just run!"

"No, I won't," cried Jade. There was

no way she was going to abandon the
White Cat.

"You must or he'll catch you. Go,
please go!"

Jade heard the desperation in his
voice. King Rat moved towards her.
She wanted to rescue the White Cat,
but she needed time to come up with a
plan.

"I'll be back!" she cried, and then she
turned and sprinted away as fast as
her feet would carry her.

# The Sylphs

Jade ran as hard as she could through the Enchanted Wood. She could still hear the urgency in the White Cat's voice, calling after her.

"No, don't go into the wood! Run away!"

But all the same, Jade thought it would be safer to stay amongst the trees, rather than be an open target for the horrid King Rat. She knew he had a sword, and his guards had lassos.

"Guards, lock that cat in the deepest dungeon! I'm going to deal with this sylph-in-disguise. I'll sniff her out!" bellowed King Rat.

Jade stumbled along, tripping over tree roots, her hair falling out of its bun, her heart thudding as she heard King Rat running after her. The poor White Cat was in terrible danger and

all because of her big mouth. She
shouldn't have gone rushing in saying
whatever she wanted. She should have
listened to him. But
what was it that
King Rat had said?
Something about
how she stood like a
ballet dancer? Jade was surprised, but
also found herself taking what he said
as a compliment.

The trees grew denser and denser as
Jade ran and yet it wasn't getting any
darker. In fact, it seemed to be lighter.

That must be the magic powers of the sylphs. So they really *did* light up the wood like the White Cat said. And what was that lovely smell? Honeysuckle? Yes, there must be a honeysuckle bush just nearby.

"You can't escape me, you stupid sylph!" King Rat's voice was slightly fainter now.

Jade ran harder than ever, following the light.

"Oh!"

A moment later she stood rooted to the spot, staring into the frightened

eyes of a beautiful
girl. Wearing a
long white ballet
dress of the
softest net, she
had wings of fine
gauze and hair that
flowed around her
shoulders. She shimmered and glowed,
balancing effortlessly on the point of
her ballet shoe. Behind her were many
more of the graceful creatures dancing.
Their white light was like a soft mist
between the dark trees.

Jade thought this was one of the most beautiful sights she had ever seen. But the magic was broken by a mocking sing-song voice. "I'm getting closer!"

*Oh no!* thought Jade, panicking. How stupid could she have been, leading King Rat straight to the sylphs! She had to put him off the scent. Right now!

Without wasting a second, Jade mouthed to the sylph in front, "Don't worry. I won't let him find you." Then she began to run with all her might

back in the direction she'd come from.

A plan formed in her mind. She would lead King Rat away from the sylphs and then jump into the honeysuckle bush. Hopefully, the strong smell of the flowers would mask her scent so that he would run straight on past – away from the sylphs!

Jade's breath came in ragged gasps, and her heart pounded. It was such a relief when she finally came across the sweetly scented honeysuckle. She dived into its leafy bushes.

And there she sat, hugging her knees tightly and trying to calm her breathing.

Through the mass of leaves she could only see one small patch of the wood. And apart from a few brittle leaves rustling, all was still.

Then a gleaming sword came into view from behind one of the trees, followed by a black rat leg. Jade's hand flew to her mouth.

# The Sylph-Child

"I know you're somewhere near!" King Rat called.

Jade's stomach turned over. She shrank back as the rat came so close to her hiding place that she could have reached out and touched him.

"I know you can hear me, wherever you are!"

Jade swallowed, but then something happened to King Rat's voice. It seemed to falter with his next words. "What's happening? Hang on! What's going on? Why is it getting dark?"

*Yes*, thought, Jade, looking round, *he's right! The light* is *fading.*

"Those wretched dancing creatures are responsible for this," spat King Rat. "Now I can't see a thing. Well, they needn't think I've finished with them!"

And with that he went stumbling off

into the darkness, his voice becoming more and more distant. "I'll get rid of the lot of you! Mark my words, I'll be back!"

Jade let out a trembling breath. She'd had a lucky escape, and now she had to get back to the sylphs. There was no one else to ask for help.

Desperately hoping she was going in the right direction, Jade crept out of her hiding place and took a few careful steps. But it was no good. She simply couldn't see. She hung her head and bit her lip, wondering where on earth to turn now, when suddenly she heard someone calling her name.

"Jade! Jade!"

Her name seemed to be floating on the softest breath of a breeze, and each time it was repeated, a little more light grew out of the darkness. Then, sweet lilting music sounded in the distance. Jade found herself drawn to it like a magnet.

The music grew stronger and the light brighter, and soon she was running. But only moments later, she stopped abruptly, feeling a wave of pure wonder wash over her. Before her eyes, the sylphs were dancing. Their long net skirts gently rose and fell as they wove smooth shimmering patterns, their graceful arms framing their faces. It was the most beautiful dance Jade had ever seen. A lump

came into her throat. So *this* was the
magic of ballet.

The leading sylph danced forwards.
"My name is Ava," she said softly.
"Thank you for not giving us away."

Jade swallowed. "I'm… I'm Jade."

"You must be from the human world." Ava nodded and smiled.

She seemed so kind and wise that Jade found herself gabbling away. "I shouldn't have rushed into the woods or talked to King Rat like I did. The White Cat was trying to warn me. And now he's been captured and taken to the dungeons. I've got to try and rescue him, but I don't have a clue where to begin."

As Jade had been talking, the other sylphs had silently gathered around Ava, nodding gravely. "We knew

something awful was happening when
we heard talk of a funfair being built."

Jade watched as the sylphs drew in
closer still to each other. They seemed
to be talking and yet their voices were
softer than whispers. Eventually they
looked back at her, and Ava spoke
again.

"We sylphs have to live amongst trees to survive. If there is a funfair we will be driven out of the wood and we will die. We must do something." She frowned. "But what?"

The other sylphs looked anxiously at each other fluttering their wings.

"It's a pity King Rat isn't afraid of anything," said Jade. "If we could just scare him then  maybe he'd leave these woods – and forget all about building a funfair."

Ava stared at her. "But that's it! That's a wonderful idea, Jade." She turned to the other sylphs. "We could scare King Rat by making him think he has seen the magical Sylph-Child."

The sylphs surrounding her gasped and nodded eagerly. Ava turned back to Jade. "The magical Sylph-Child is believed to be the sylphs' supreme ruler, although no one living has ever seen her. Legend has it that she sleeps deep in the heart of the wood. It is said that if she is annoyed, she will awake and cause great harm. If I cast a spell to make you look like one of us, you could be mistaken for the Sylph-Child. Then, if King Rat and his guards saw you, hopefully they would be very afraid. The question is, do you want to take the risk of seeing King Rat again?"

Jade's heart beat faster. "Yes," she whispered. "I just want to rescue the White Cat – and stop King Rat building a funfair if I can."

Ava gave her a warm look. "You are very brave. King Rat will have gone back to his castle now. I will use my magic to take you right inside it. You

must then find your way to where the
White Cat is imprisoned, taking care
not to let the guards see you. At the
last possible moment you must appear
before them, as if out of thin air.
Hopefully that will scare them off and
give you time to release your friend."

Ava smiled and Jade tried a shaky
smile back. It all felt like such a big
responsibility.

"Thank you," she murmured as she
stood in the middle of the circle of
sylphs as instructed.

The wings of the sylphs rose up in a

single wave, and a pure white mist
filled the circle, wrapping around Jade.
She felt her feet leave the
ground and for a
moment she seemed
to be floating.
Then she landed
on cold grey
flagstones, and
shivered, partly
with shock, partly at
feeling so alone.

She looked down. In her long floaty
white dress she felt so much more like

a real ballet dancer. Her straight hair
hung in a heavy curtain down her
back, and when she reached
behind, she touched silky
wings. Glancing
around she saw she
was inside the great
hall of a castle.
There were pictures
of King Rat on the
walls and a staircase
down that was marked with
the word 'Dungeons'. For a moment,
Jade wished she was somewhere –

*anywhere* – else. She took a deep breath.

"Now concentrate!" she told herself firmly as she moved towards some wide granite steps and began to go down them on shaky legs.

The air was
growing colder
and every
ten steps
there was a
sharp angle
that lead to
the next ten,
like a spiral staircase

74

with no curves.

The bottom stair led to a dark passage where a single pair of heavy boots could be heard clomping back and forth. *At least that meant there was only one guard*, thought Jade, her heart hammering.

She waited, pressing her back against the wall, hidden from sight. Then as soon as she heard the footsteps heading away from her, she stepped into the passage and silently crept up behind the unsuspecting guard. At the very end he turned. And when he saw

Jade, a look of terror came into his eyes.

"Oh, you're... No, you can't be...
the... "

Jade felt terrified at that point too.
She had no idea how the Sylph-Child
might talk. So she just kept silent and
fixed her hardest stare on the mouse
guard while she tried to imagine that
she really *was* the supreme leader of
the sylphs.

"Yes," she said, trying to make her
voice sound like a sylph. "I am the
Sylph-Child. And I command you to
release the White Cat immediately."

Jade hadn't rehearsed those words
and yet they must have sounded all
right because the trembling guard
looked very scared. "But... but... if I
do, King Rat will have me thrown in
the dungeons!" he stammered.

"If you don't, you'll have *me* to deal with!" Jade told him. She stared at him. "You don't want to see me angry, do you?"

To her delight, the guard gulped and began to unclip a heavy set of keys from his belt. "No, Your Majesty... I mean yes, Your Majesty... well, anything you say, Your Majesty."

He took a step forward

then hesitated, his knees knocking together and Jade realised he was actually too scared to pass her.

"Thank you," she said, trying not to grin as she stepped smoothly to one side, then followed him and his jangling keys as he walked shakily down the passage.

Around a corner, more stairs descended even deeper. Jade let the guard lead the way, trying not to shiver as the ice-cold air enveloped her.

"This is… the cell," he stammered,

winding his tail round and round in his hands.

"Unlock the door!" she commanded.

"Yes, Your Greatness," replied the guard, which suddenly made Jade want to giggle. But she kept her poise and her powerful gaze in place right up until the White Cat stepped out of his cell and stood beside her.

"This is the Sylph-Child," the mouse guard whispered.

Poor White Cat looked most confused and alarmed himself. "Oh, my ears and whiskers! Oh, my sparkling eyes!"

He sank into a deep bow. He didn't
appear to recognise her at all, which
was good. It would be terrible if he
gave the game away by mistake.

"Come," Jade instructed him in her
new regal voice. Then she turned to the

guard. "You will remain here until you are told otherwise."

"Oh, yes please!" cried the guard in relief as he ran into the dungeon, slamming the door shut behind him.

Silently, Jade led the White Cat up the stairs. It wasn't until they reached the third flight that she turned to him and whispered, "It's me! Jade! The sylphs had this idea for me to pretend to be the Sylph-Child and rescue you."

The White Cat gave a start as he peered more closely at her, then he

gave a miaow and hugged her tight.
"Oh, my goodness. You clever, clever
thing!!"

"And now I must fool King Rat,"
said Jade, slightly fearfully. "If I can
scare him too, I might be able to stop
him from going ahead with this funfair
idea."

"What a brilliant idea!" said the White Cat, patting her arm encouragingly.

"But what if King Rat recognises me? He's seen me close up, after all," Jade said.

"Well, you managed to fool *me*!" chuckled the White Cat. "Just act exactly as you did in the dungeon! Listen, he's coming. I'll see you outside!" And with that the White Cat leaped through an open window and Jade quickly darted behind a curtain.

"Guards!" King Rat sounded as

though he was in a very bad mood.
"Bring me torches and lamps. We're
returning to the wood. I want that girl
caught, and to be rid of those stupid
sylph creatures once and for all!"

Jade knew she must act immediately.
With her heart beating wildly, she
stepped out from behind the curtain.

# The Promise

A cold fear enveloped Jade as King Rat swung round and saw her there.

"Who are you?" he snarled, taking a step forward. "How did you get into my castle?"

Jade tried to ignore the butterflies

swarming in her stomach, and concentrated on staying perfectly still. She didn't waver from his gaze, but fixed him with round, staring eyes.

"Well?" This time his voice sounded less sure of itself.

Silence had worked with the guard. So Jade made herself count to ten inside her head, before she began to speak. Her tone was low and even. "I am the Sylph-Child. I am here because you have broken the law of the Enchanted Wood."

There was another short silence then

King Rat's eyes suddenly filled with terror. He began hopping from foot to foot like a little child being told off. "I... I..."

Jade lifted her chin. "You *what*?" she demanded in the coldest voice she could muster.

King Rat started bowing and grovelling, bending so low his whiskers touched the dusty floor. "I beg you...

…have mercy upon me, oh mighty Sylph-Child. Please, please. I'll do *anything.*"

It was all Jade could do not to punch the air, and shout, "Yes, I did it!", but she knew that if she let her mask slip, even for a second, she would be in grave danger. So she took care to keep her tone steady. "Very well. I will be merciful, if you take an oath!" she went on, wishing she'd had more time to prepare her words.

"Anything, Your Royal Sylphness!" said King Rat dropping to his knees and holding up his paws. "Oh, please don't hurt me!"

"You must go immediately to the Enchanted Wood and take down the sign you hung there," commanded Jade. "Then you must announce to the people of Enchantia that the wood will remain exactly as it is, for ever."

"Yes, yes, oh Majestic One!" the King promised, nodding as hard as he could, his words falling over each other. "I will do just as you say. Exactly as you want. I will, I will, I will!"

But Jade knew that she hadn't asked enough of him. She had to be quite sure the wicked rodent would never break his promise.

"And finally…" she said, taking a step forward and deepening her tone, "if *ever* it should come to my ears that you have broken this promise, I shall show *no mercy*. Do you understand?"

King Rat was positively cowering.
"Yes, yes! I understand, Your Greatness!"

"Then arise and be gone to the
Enchanted Wood immediately!"

He didn't need telling twice. In a
flash the nasty rat was out of his front
door, running for his life towards the
Enchanted Wood.

A few moments later, the White Cat
and Jade high-fived each other in the
grounds of King Rat's castle.

"Oh, my glittering eyes!" laughed

92

the White Cat. "I heard it all through the window from my hiding place behind a wall. You did a grand job!"

Jade grinned happily. "Can you magic us back to the Enchanted Wood? I'm dying to hear what King Rat has to say!"

"Absolutely," came the reply, as the

White Cat drew a circle on the ground with his tail.

A moment later he and Jade were whisked away in a shower of silver sparkles.

"Look, the sign's already gone!" Jade whispered excitedly as they alighted at the edge of the wood.

"But listen!" said the White Cat. "King Rat is addressing everyone right now!"

Jade and the White Cat hid behind a

tree. Peeping out
cautiously, Jade
saw that there
were many
others
gathered
round.

  "I have
changed my mind
about the funfair!" King Rat
announced pompously. "A king has
the right to change his mind,
obviously." He looked around wildly,
as though he feared the Sylph-Child

might be listening. "Did you… er,
hear that? No funfair or *any* building
at all *ever* in the Enchanted Wood.
I… er… I give you my word!"

The moment his speech was finished
he turned from the crowds and took
flight. Jade clapped her hand over her
mouth so the giggles couldn't escape
and the White Cat's eyes twinkled with
amusement. Then the wood suddenly
erupted with the sound of loud
cheering and clapping. And as music
filled the air, everyone began to dance.

The White Cat took Jade's hands in
his paws and spun her round. "You
did it! You really did it!"

Jade felt so happy watching
everyone. Whenever anyone looked at

her quizzically, the White Cat

explained that she was a special guest

from the human world who had

helped them in their time of need.

Then Jade's back was patted and her hand shaken over and over again by many of Enchantia's characters. It gave her such a contented feeling.

"What kind of dancing do you like best?" the White Cat asked her after a while.

"Oh, I like str..." Jade stopped in confusion. Of course it was true, she absolutely loved street dancing. But now she loved ballet too.

She never did answer that question though, because people were beckoning her over. "Come and join the celebrations!" they cried, pulling her into the circle. "You too, White Cat!"

Jade loved every second of the dancing. The white light from the sylphs filtered through the trees and created the most breathtaking atmosphere.

"You see," said the White Cat,

coming to stand beside Jade after an energetic *pas de chat*, "the Enchanted Wood really does inspire people."

Jade nodded hard. "It certainly does," she said, with a sigh of pleasure. "You were so right, White Cat. I can feel it myself. I didn't know what I was talking about before. The bright lights of a funfair are nothing compared to the sylphs' pure light."

"And what about this little light?" smiled the White Cat, nodding his head at Jade's shoes.

Jade followed his gaze and saw with

a start that her red shoes were glowing brightly. "Does that mean it's time for me to go?" she asked.

The White Cat smiled and nodded.

"It was lovely to meet you, White Cat," said Jade, feeling suddenly a bit shy.

"And you too," replied the White Cat. Then he bowed low and came up grinning. "Thank you once more for your help! Come and see us again soon."

"How?" Jade asked, but she didn't have time to ask further as her feet really were tingling. "Say goodbye to the sylphs for me," she said instead. The glowing shoes began to sparkle, and the sparkles turned to a mass of colours that swirled around Jade's feet.

Just before Jade was lifted up and whisked away, a gentle whisper came to her ears, as if from deep in the wood. "Thank you for saving our Enchanted Wood."

Jade's heart sang.

"Goodbye! Goodbye!"

# The Magic of Ballet

Jade looked down at her feet and smiled.
Her little red shoes were still on, but she
was back standing in the corridor outside
the studio at Madame Za-Za's in her
normal ballet outfit. She touched her
hair. A few strands had escaped, but

it was mainly in the bun.

What a time she'd had in Enchantia! The thought made her eyes fly open in alarm. Everyone in class must be wondering where on earth she'd got to. She could hear music from the other side of the door. Strangely, it sounded like the same music that had been playing when she left the room, but it couldn't be, could it?

It took quite a lot of courage to go back in because everyone was bound to stare at her.

"Oh well, here goes!" she whispered

under her breath.

But no one looked at her as she took her place in the row. And even more oddly, they were still doing the same exercise as before.

"That was quick!" whispered the girl standing next to her, throwing Jade a smile.

Jade frowned. *Quick*? She looked up at the clock. It said ten twenty-nine. That was amazing! No time at all had passed in the real world while she'd been away in Enchantia.

"Stretch the supporting leg, Jade, and frame the head with the arm." Jade did as she was told.

"Lovely!" There was a note of something that Jade hadn't heard before in Madame Za-Za's voice.

"Look in the mirror, my dear."

Again Jade did as she was told. *Is that really me?* she thought. The girls on either side of her were both smiling at her and one of them mouthed, "Really good!"

Jade's heart soared. She lowered her arm with the music and imitated the movements that the other girls were doing to form a new shape. Her arms felt a little stiff so she softened them and turned out her supporting leg.

When she looked up, Madame Za-Za's

appraising gaze was upon her. She nodded at Jade, her eyes full of warmth. "Well done!"

*I belong here,* thought Jade. *I actually feel as if I belong in this ballet class. But why? What's happened? Have I somehow been touched by the magic of the sylphs? No, maybe it isn't that,* she realised. *Maybe it's simply the magic of ballet!*

For a second in the mirror, it was as though Jade was looking at a beautiful misty glade filled with dancing shimmering white light. She smiled and danced on. She'd had one adventure in Enchantia. When would the next one begin?

*Tiptoe over the page to learn*

*a special dance step...*

# Darcey's Magical Masterclass

## Battement fondu

*This exercise will help you to learn how music and ballet work together and how to express the music through your dancing.*

**1.**
Start by standing in fifth position with your arm in preparatory position.

**2.**
Move your arm through preparatory position. Also lift your right foot slowly off the floor and begin to bend both knees.

**3.**
*Demi-plié* with your left leg and *coup de pied* with your right with pointed toe. Turn out both your legs as much as possible.

**4.**
Open your right leg and slowly stretch your supporting left leg whilst moving your right arm to second position.

**5.**
Hold your left arm and leg both in second position, looking straight ahead. Balance and stretch out as far as you can.

**6.**
Lower your right leg and arm back into fifth position. You can do this to the front and back as well.

Everyone in Enchantia is planning the

perfect party, but guests keep

disappearing!

Read on for a sneak preview

of Jade's next adventure...

° ⊙ ˙* ☆ ⊙ ˙* ☆ ⊙ ˙* ☆ ⊙ ˙* ° ⊙

As Jade was set down in a village square, she stared around her.

"I'm back!" she breathed happily. "This *is* Enchantia!"

"Jade! Jade!" called a familiar voice. The White Cat was running up to her. "Lovely day!"

Jade hugged her friend. "It's great to see you again. You look happy, Cat!"

"Well, thank you!" her friend replied with a chuckle, sweeping off his top hat in a grand gesture and bowing low. Then he straightened up smartly, leaned forwards and spoke in a low voice. "I think there's er… something rather… odd going on though, Jade."

"Odd?" said Jade, feeling curious.

"Yes, very odd!" replied the cat, looking a bit embarrassed. "You see, I keep coming across people standing in huddles and talking in whispers. But the moment I ask what's going on, they just say, 'Oh nothing!' and leave me none the wiser!"

Jade wrinkled her nose. "That does sound a bit

weird!" she agreed. And straight after she spoke, as if
from nowhere, there was a tiny flash. "Oh! What was
that?"

"Exactly!" her friend replied, sweeping the air with
his paw. "I *knew* I hadn't been imagining those little
flashes I keep seeing! And yet whenever I mention them
to anyone, they look at me as though I've gone mad!"

The White Cat shook his head, baffled, and Jade
laughed.

A moment later her laughter stopped and her hand
flew to her mouth. From out of a hazy mist, before her
very eyes, appeared the most beautiful ballerina. And
not just any ballerina – it was the one Jade had just
been reading about, the Lilac Fairy from *Sleeping
Beauty*.

"Hello," said the fairy in a tinkly voice. "I'm Lila."

"Hello… Lila." Jade couldn't help staring at the
fairy's sparkling lilac tutu and her beautiful wings that
fluttered and shimmered with the palest shades of the
rainbow. On her head a diamond tiara sparkled, and in
her hand she held a delicate wand.

"Lila, meet Jade!" the White Cat introduced her. Then he turned with concern to the fairy. "What is it, Lila? You look worried."

"We need your help, White Cat. One of the gingerbread children has climbed too high in the tree beside the green, and now she's completely stuck and getting upset."

"Don't worry! I'm on my way!" said the White Cat and he bounded off lightly and quickly.

Jade felt a bit tongue-tied in the presence of the Lilac Fairy, but she didn't need to say anything. Lila had already taken a small step closer and was talking urgently.

"It's true there *is* a gingerbread child stuck up a tree, but she's a very good climber and is only pretending to be stuck so I could talk to you alone."

Jade's eyes widened. "Oh!"

"You see, it's the White Cat's birthday today…"

**To be continued…**

# The Story of Giselle

Giselle lived with her mum in a little thatched cottage in the middle of their village. More than anything else in the world Giselle loved to dance. Sometimes her mum would get cross with her. "Too much dancing will make you tired," she scolded. But Giselle just laughed and spun away to practise her steps.

A boy named Loys had just moved to the village. Nobody knew very much about him, but everybody liked him. He liked watching Giselle's dances and soon they fell in love.

But Loys wasn't the only person who loved Giselle. The local gamekeeper Hilarion had been friends with her since they were little. He wanted to marry her one day. He was jealous of Loys and he didn't trust him. "There is something strange about him," he thought. "He is not like the rest of the villagers."

One day, when nobody was looking, Hilarion crept quietly into Loys's cottage. Inside, he found a long velvet cloak and a glittering silver sword. They looked like they belonged to a very rich person. "Aha," he thought, "now I know his secret…"

Outside in the square, there was lots of noise and excitement. A prince and his beautiful daughter had stopped to rest in the village and a big crowd had come running to see them. Giselle couldn't stop staring at their colourful silk clothes and shining, golden jewellery.

"Don't just stand there, silly," said her mum. "I expect our guests would like something to eat and drink."

Giselle felt a bit shy as she helped her mum bring out trays of food but the prince's daughter smiled kindly at her, "My name's Bathilde," she said, "What's yours?"

Soon the two of them were chattering away and laughing together. Giselle even showed Bathilde a few of her dance steps. "Oh! I wish you could come and live with me at the palace," said Bathilde. "We'd have so much fun."

"That would be lovely," agreed Giselle, "but I'm getting married soon to a boy from the village."

Just at that moment they heard angry voices. Hilarion was arguing with Loys and waving a cloak and sword in the air. Giselle ran over to them.

"What's the matter?" she asked.

Hilarion explained that the sword and cloak belonged to a man called Duke Albrecht. Loys wasn't really a village boy – he was the Duke in disguise! Someone royal like that would never be able to marry a peasant girl like Giselle.

"Is that true?" asked Giselle. Loys just hung his head and looked uncomfortable but Bathilde spoke instead.

"Yes," she answered sadly, "he is really Duke Albrecht, and what's more, he is engaged to marry me!"

At this horrible news Giselle burst into tears. "I will go to the forest and live with the sylphs," she sobbed. Everybody gasped. The sylphs were the spirits of girls who had had their hearts broken. They were beautiful, but dangerous. Before anyone could stop her, Giselle ran towards the forest crying.

It was dark in the forest and Giselle was

frightened. But then a faint light started to glow among the trees. At first Giselle thought it was just the moon, but then she saw that it was ghostly, dancing girls. They were wearing shimmering, white dresses and had delicate wings on their backs. It was the sylphs. Giselle thought they were the most beautiful sight she had ever seen. "Come and join us in our dance," they called to her. Giselle and the sylphs twirled and spun in a wonderful moonlit dance. Giselle forgot about being sad and started to enjoy herself. But then over the magical music she heard Loys calling her name. He had come to find her to say sorry. Giselle was ready to forgive him, but the sylphs were cross that he had made their new friend so sad.

"We will take him to our queen who will keep him prisoner in the deep, dark forest for ever," they said. They danced around the terrified Loys, pulling at him with their ghostly white fingers.

Giselle was still a little bit cross with Loys, but she didn't want him to be taken prisoner. She whirled between the sylphs and held his hand. "Dance with me," she told him. Giselle and Loys danced a beautiful *pas de deux* – a dance for two – moving slowly through the forest. When the dance ended Loys saw that Giselle had brought him to the edge of the trees. The sun was shining and Loys was safe. He wanted Giselle to come back to the village, but she shook her head.

"I'm happy here with the sylphs," she said. Then with a last wave goodbye, she spun off into the forest to dance with her new friends.

*Meet another girl in Enchantia over the page…*

Hi, my name's Holly and I love ballet more than anything. Dancing makes me think of my mum because she's a professional dancer. I love the emotions and stories in ballet, sometimes I get so carried away I forget where I am! Luckily I'm always in the best places: dancing at Madame Za-Za's or in Enchantia The White Cat and I have done so much there: protecting Cinderella from an evil magician, reuniting Beauty and the Beast, and even making things right in the Land of Sweets!

**Hair colour:** Dark brown

**Eye colour:** Green

**Likes:** Expressing myself through dancing

**Dislikes:** Feeling left out

**Favourite ballet:** Sleeping Beauty (particularly the Rose Adagio dance)

**Best friend in Enchantia:** The White Cat

Read all my Magic Ballerina adventures...

# Darcey Bussell

Buy more great Magic Ballerina books direct from HarperCollins
at 10% off recommended retail price.
FREE postage and packing in the UK.

Jade and the Enchanted Wood     ISBN   978 0 00 734875 6

Jade and the Surprise Party     ISBN   978 0 00 734876 3

Jade and the Silver Flute     ISBN   978 0 00 734877 0

Jade and the Carnival     ISBN   978 0 00 734878 7

All priced at £3.99